MUMMY
CAT

by MARCUS EWERT
Illustrations by LISA BROWN

CLARION BOOKS   HOUGHTON MIFFLIN HARCOURT
BOSTON   NEW YORK

The winds hiss over desert sand.
The moon shines down on empty land.
And long ago . . .

. . . the pharaohs hid
their treasures in this pyramid.

Deep within this maze of stone,
a creature wakes up, all alone.

For the first time
in a hundred years,
he shakes off dust.
He flicks his ears.

From head to tail, dry strips
of cloth softly russssstle,
like a moth.

A CAT
who moves without a breath:
a *mummy cat,* who's passed through Death.

And one cold night, each century,
he gets up, and he checks to see

if *she's* come back, his loving friend . . .
so that this lonely time can end.

For she was the girl-queen, Hat-shup-set!
And he'd been her *hero,* not just her pet!

The *boldest* cat ancient Egypt had seen—
the number-one cat: the cat of the *queen!*

But now? He just feels old, and small.
He shuffles slowly down the hall.

And all around are painted scenes
of his past life, with Egypt's queen.

Mummy Cat purrs to see the smile
of the young girl playing by the Nile.

Two boats floated,
but one ship sank—

clawed by the cat on the riverbank!

Or this mural of a noontime nap:
dreams of mice, on the queen's own lap.

Their couch was set beside the pool.
The shade from date trees kept them cool.

Here's Hat-shup-set drawing,
with her palette of inks.
And here he is posing: a miniature sphinx!

Marvelous scenes of the way things *were*,
When Mummy Cat was alive, with *her*.

But the very next picture makes Mummy Cat wail:
the queen struck down by a

SCORPION'S TAIL!

Mummy Cat knows he's not to blame—
but he couldn't save her, all the same.
The scorpion struck both her and him;

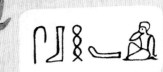

the poison spread from limb to limb.

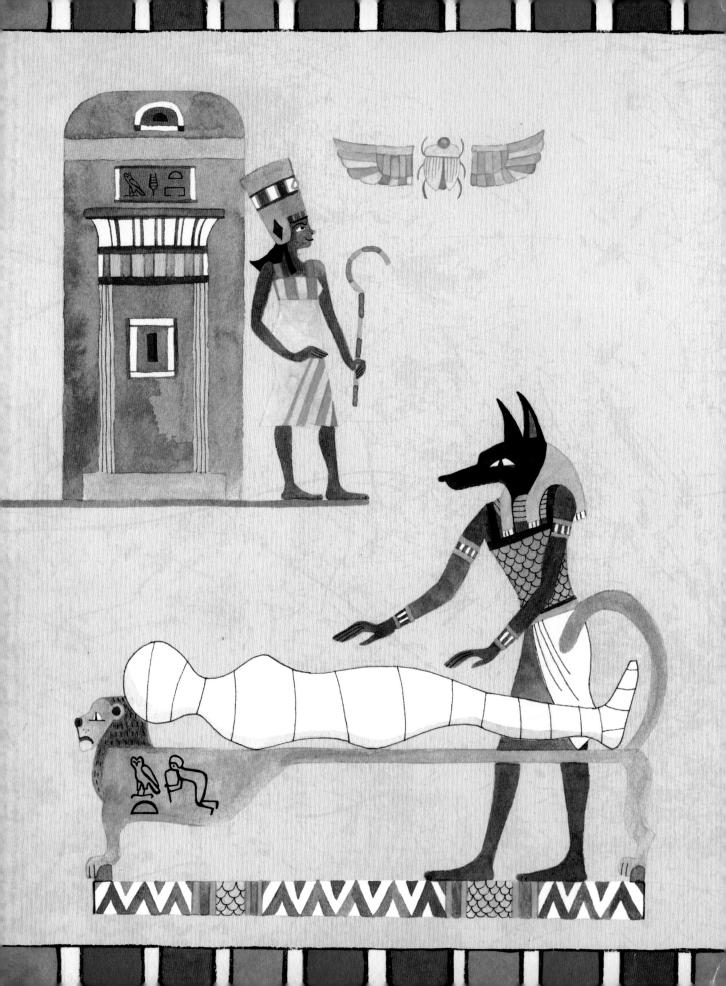

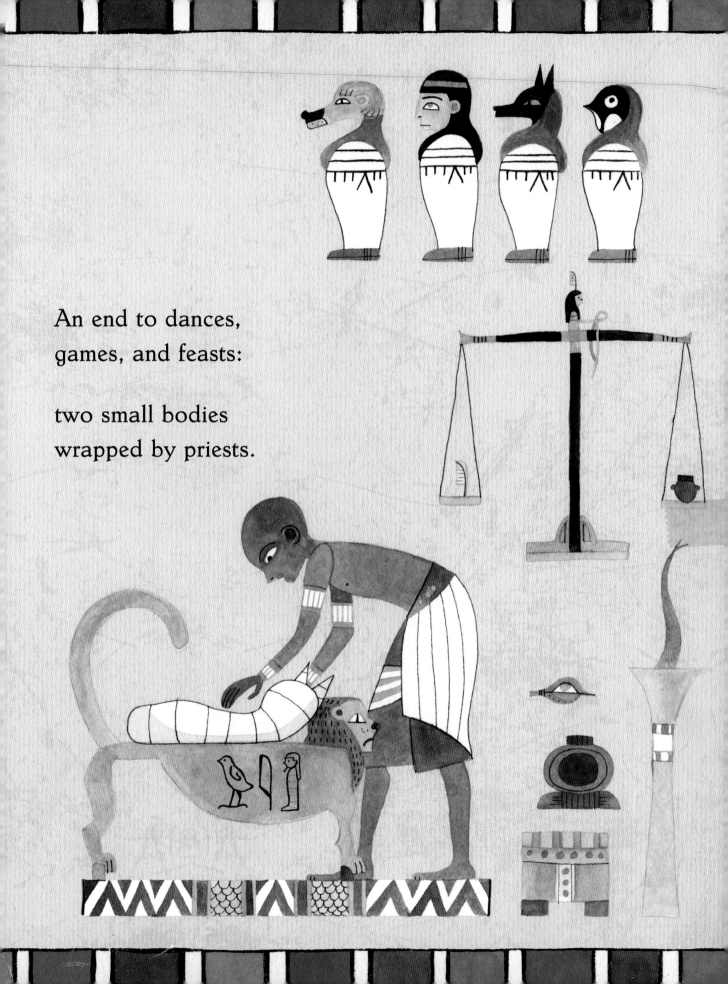

An end to dances,
games, and feasts:

two small bodies
wrapped by priests.

The paintings stop. The cat's alone
with silence, dust, and dull gray stone.

Mummy Cat slumps a little more.
But up ahead . . . there is a door.

And through that door, there is a room—
the very center of the tomb.
A chamber stuffed with lovely things:

a crown, a throne, four golden rings,
mirrors, dolls, and makeup kits . . .
Nothing that matters the slightest bit.

Nothing that matters . . . except for the queen,
her face on the coffin, smiling, serene.

This cold, golden coffin—is this all he gets?
Where is the girl he can never forget?

Will *tonight* be the night that she comes back?
Will the coffin open, even a crack?

He'll wait, he'll wait, till his friend reappears:
the queen of his heart . . .

. . . for three thousand years.

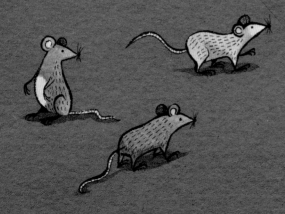

MUMMIES, CATS, QUEENS, AND HIEROGLYPHS

MUMMIES

Egypt is a hot, dry country. Things that would rot quickly anywhere else—for instance, anything made from bits of plants and animals—might last a *very* long time in Egypt. Wood, paper, leather, cloth, and rope—these can all endure for thousands of years. The hot desert sands can even preserve a dead body by drying it out completely. Perhaps this is where the ancient Egyptians got the idea to mummify their dead.

To mummify a dead body means to specially prepare, dry, and preserve it. For a poor person in ancient Egypt, mummification might be as simple as burying a dead body in a hole lined with rocks, and trusting the desert to do the rest. A rich person, on the other hand, might build what amounted to an entire house for their dead loved one, complete with furniture and beautifully painted walls. The mummification of someone like the pharaoh (the ruler of ancient Egypt) often took *weeks,* with priests chanting spells and special craftspeople performing delicate operations. For example, the mummy's liver, lungs, and stomach all had to be removed and placed in their own special jars. (The brain, however, was *not* put in a jar. Typically, it was removed through the nostrils . . . and thrown away!) The inside of the body would be washed with wine, spices, and salt before the corpse was closed up again. Last of all, the mummy was wrapped from head to toe with strips of cloth. Only then was the dead person ready for the long journey into the afterlife.

The Ancient Egyptians had many different beliefs about souls and the afterlife, but generally they believed that a properly mummified person would spend eternity enjoying the things with which he or she had been buried. A poor person's grave might hold only a few loaves of bread and some fish to eat, while a pharaoh's tomb might contain (in addition to food): furniture, clothing, wigs, makeup, perfume, jewelry, board games, harps, flower bouquets, pens, ink, statues, weapons, fans, chariots . . . even boats! Artists painted murals inside the tombs that showed the dead person doing the things he or she liked most in life, whether that was dancing, playing, hunting, or just relaxing with friends and family. The Ancient Egyptians believed that beautiful paintings like these would allow their souls to experience life's delights, forever.

CATS

The Ancient Egyptians loved and respected cats.
There was a goddess named Bastet who had a
cat's head instead of a human one, and there
were ancient temples in which *hundreds* of cats
were allowed to walk around freely. Some cats
even had pierced ears and wore gold hoop ear-
rings! And sometimes an especially beloved cat
was mummified when it died, just like a human.
This way, the cat could spend eternity with the
person who'd loved it.

HAT-SHUP-SET

There *was* an ancient queen named Hatshepsut,
a powerful woman who ruled Egypt as pharaoh
in her own right, and not merely as the wife
of a king. The historicial Hatshepsut reigned
for more than twenty years and accomplished
great things. The inspiration for the girl-queen
in *Mummy Cat* came from this proud and
remarkable woman.

HIEROGLYPHS

The Ancient Egyptians used a system of writing
called hieroglyphs, in which pictures could stand
for letters, sounds, words, or ideas.

Each of the following sets of hieroglyphs occurs within the pages of *Mummy Cat.* Can you find them all?

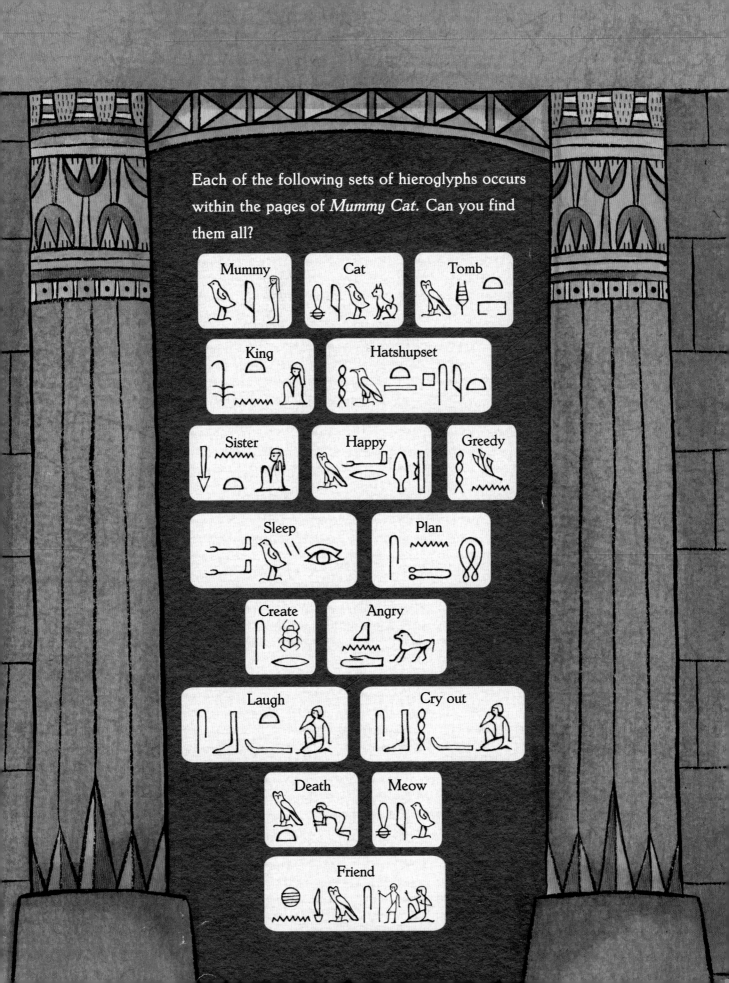

Mummy

Cat

Tomb

King

Hatshupset

Sister

Happy

Greedy

Sleep

Plan

Create

Angry

Laugh

Cry out

Death

Meow

Friend

Our thanks to J. G. Manning, the William K. and Marilyn M. Simpson Professor
of Classics and History at Yale University, for double-checking our hieroglyphics.
Any remaining errors are ours.

—M.E. & L.B.

Clarion Books
215 Park Avenue South
New York, New York 10003

Clarion Books is an imprint of
Houghton Mifflin Harcourt Publishing Company.

www.hmhco.com

The illustrations in this book were done in ink, gouache,
and watercolor on paper with digital collage.
The text was set in Dutch Mediaeval.

Library of Congress Cataloging-in-Publication Data is available.
ISBN 978-0-544-34082-4

Manufactured in China
SCP 10 9 8 7 6 5 4 3 2 1
4500525481

To Rhoda and Barbara, our mummies.

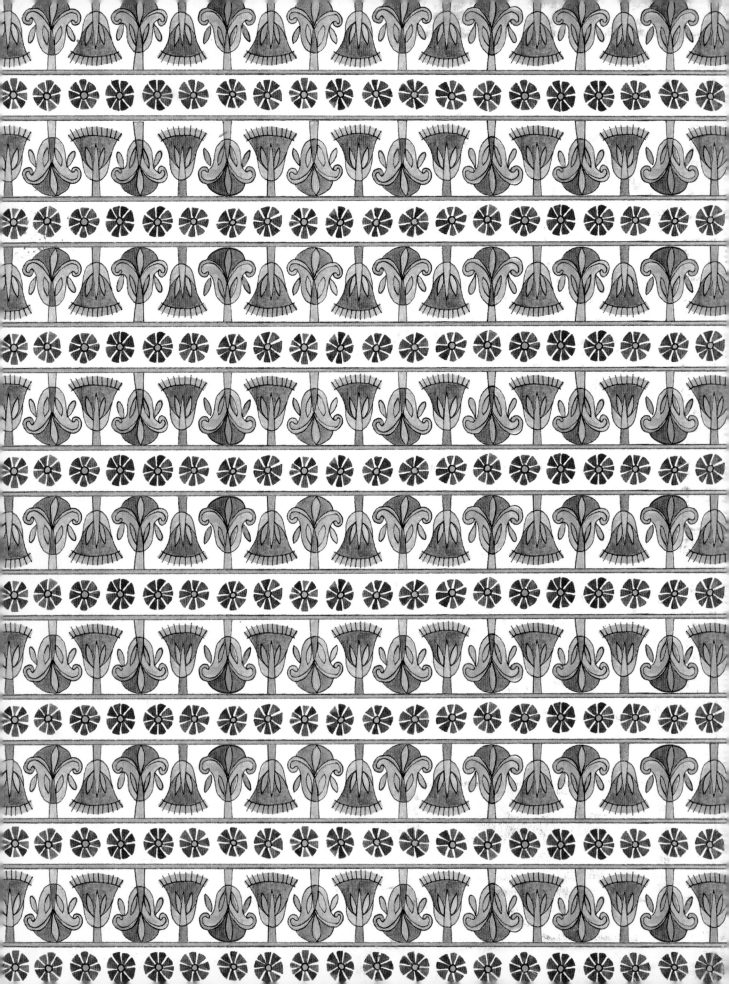